CLASSIC FAIRY TALES

Little Red RIDING HOOD

Retold by Sam McBratney

Illustrated by Emma Chichester Clark

MACDONALD YOUNG BOOKS

First published in Great Britain in 1996
by Macdonald Young Books
61 Western Road
Hove
East Sussex BN3 1JD

Designed by Shireen Nathoo Design

Typeset in 20pt Minion
Printed and bound in Belgium by Proost International Book Co.

British Library Cataloguing in Publication Data available.

ISBN: 0 7500 2002 4
ISBN: 0 7500 2003 2 (pb)

Once upon a time there was a little girl who lived in a house at the edge of the woods. When she went out to play, or walked down to the village, she loved to wear the red cape that her grandma had made for her. People were so used to seeing the little girl in the red cape that they called her 'Little Red Riding Hood'.

Two or three times each week, Little Red Riding Hood and her mother went to visit Grandma. Always keeping to the main path, they walked quickly through the woods to Grandma's house. The main path was bright and open, and well away from the shadows of the trees, where there were dark and lonely places.

Grandma lived by herself. She was pleased to get the basket of food that they brought, but most of all she liked to see Little Red Riding Hood.

"My goodness, how you're growing," she would say. "Soon you'll be too big for the red cape I made you!"

One day, Little Red Riding Hood's mother was too busy to visit Grandma.

"I could go by myself," said Little Red Riding Hood. "Please let me go – Grandma will wonder why we didn't come today."

"Will you promise to walk quickly through the woods without stopping?" said her mother.

"Yes."

"And will you keep to the main path where it's bright and open?"

"Indeed I will," promised Little Red Riding Hood.

So Little Red Riding Hood set off for Grandma's house with her basket of bread, some butter and some honey. On her way through the woods she didn't stop to listen to the birds singing. And she didn't stop to watch the squirrels playing in the trees, even though watching squirrels was a thing she liked to do.

Suddenly, in the middle part of the woods where the trees grew especially tall, everything went silent. The birds no longer sang their songs, and Little Red Riding Hood wondered where the squirrels had gone. And why was the wood suddenly so quiet and still? Then she saw someone looking out from behind a bush.

It was a wolf. No one had ever told Little Red Riding Hood about wolves. No one had ever told her that a little girl on her own is exactly what a hungry wolf is looking for, and so she was not a bit afraid when he said, "Hello".

"Hello," she replied. "I'm sorry but I'm not allowed to stop. My mother said I must walk quickly through the woods."

"Never mind, I shall walk quickly, too," smiled the wolf. "What's in your basket?"

"Some bread and honey for my grandma. She lives on her own, you see, and we bring her things to eat. Do you like honey?"

The wolf glanced sideways at Little Red Riding Hood. "It's not what I like best," he said quietly.

"Would you like me to show you something that all grandmothers love? It's just over there among the trees."

What could he mean? Little Red Riding
Hood did not want to leave the main path
where it was bright and open; but it would be
wonderful to have a surprise to give to
Grandma. So she followed the wolf into the
trees, and he showed her a place where
bluebells grew.

"Oh, they're lovely flowers!" cried Little
Red Riding Hood.

"They are," said the wolf, "they are lovely
flowers. And they don't belong to anyone.
Why don't you stop and pick some for your
grandmother?"

The wolf watched Little Red Riding Hood
pick a bluebell here and a bluebell there; and
as he watched, he thought that this would be
a good time and a very good place to eat her
– now that she was away from the main path.
But he was a crafty wolf, and soon thought
of a better idea. He could have two meals
instead of one.

"If you tell me where your grandmother
lives," he said, "perhaps I could visit her, too."

So Little Red Riding Hood, who thought she had no reason to fear the wolf, told him that her grandma lived in the cottage with two chimneys beside the crooked bridge.

"Ah," said the wolf, smiling as he waved goodbye. "I have to go now, my little one, but perhaps we'll meet again soon – who knows?"

Then he ran off as quickly as he could to find the cottage with two chimneys beside the crooked bridge.

After some time Little Red Riding Hood came to her grandma's house, and knocked at the door.

"I'm in my bed, dear," said a hoarse voice, "just lift the latch and come in."

Little Red Riding Hood lifted the latch and went in, thinking that her Grandma must have a very sore throat. The curtains were drawn, and so there was very little light in the small room. The only sign of Grandma was her bonnet above the blankets.

"It's very dark in your house today, Grandma," said Little Red Riding Hood.

"I'm not well, my dear. Come over here where I can see you," whispered the hoarse voice.

As Little Red Riding Hood came closer,
she remembered the flowers in her basket. If
Grandma had a nasty cold, the bluebells
would help to cheer her up.

"I've got a lovely surprise for you,
Grandma," said Little Red Riding Hood.

"Get up on the bed and show it to me, my dear," whispered the hoarse voice.

As Little Red Riding Hood came closer still, she saw that Grandma didn't look like herself at all! She must be feeling really ill.

"Grandma, what big ears you've got," she said.

"All the better to hear you with, my dear."

"Grandma, what big eyes you've got," said Little Red Riding Hood.

"All the better to see you with, my dear."

"And Grandma, what big teeth you've got."

"All the better to eat you with!" cried the wolf, and he gobbled her up there and then.

Out in the woods, a woodcutter was on his way home for lunch. As he crossed the crooked bridge he heard a strange noise coming from the cottage, and he wondered if the old lady who lived there was all right.

Rushing in to see what was happening, the woodcutter found a wicked-looking wolf with a full belly lying in the bed.

With one blow of his axe, he killed it stone dead.

Then he cut open the wolf, and out came
a surprised and very frightened little girl. It
was Little Red Riding Hood.

"Where's my Grandma?" she asked.

At first the woodcutter feared that the wolf had eaten the old woman, too, but they soon found her, tied up in a cupboard.

"He tied me up when he heard you coming, dear," cried Grandma, as she gave Little Red Riding Hood a great big hug. "Oh, but he was a bad one! Your mother will be so glad we're safe and well."

From that day on, Little Red Riding Hood never stopped to pick flowers as she hurried through the woods. She wouldn't stop to talk to anyone. And she always kept to the main path, out in the bright and open.

31

Other titles available in the Classic Fairy Tales series:

Cinderella
Retold by Adèle Geras   Illustrated by Gwen Tourret

The Ugly Ducking
Retold by Sally Grindley   Illustrated by Bert Kitchen

Beauty and the Beast
Retold by Philippa Pearce   Illustrated by James Mayhew

Little Red Riding Hood
Retold by Sam McBratney   Illustrated by Emma Chichester Clark

Rapunzel
Retold by James Reeves   Illustrated by Sophie Allsopp

Jack and the Beanstalk
Retold by Josephine Poole   Illustrated by Paul Hess

Snow White and the Seven Dwarfs
Retold by Jenny Koralek   Illustrated by Susan Scott

Hansel and Gretel
Retold by Joyce Dunbar   Illustrated by Ian Penney

Thumbelina
Retold by Jenny Nimmo   Illustrated by Phillida Gili

Snow-White and Rose-Red
Retold by Antonia Barber   Illustrated by Gilly Marklew

Sleeping Beauty
Retold by Ann Turnbull   Illustrated by Sophy Williams

Rumplestiltskin
Retold by Helen Cresswell   Illustrated by John Howe

Goldilocks and the Three Bears
Retold by Penelope Lively   Illustrated by Debi Gliori